Dedication

I dedicate this book to my five children. Blair, Berkley, Owen, Cole and Carson — you are my inspiration. I have always tried to teach you through quality literature and engrain a love of books. You are my greatest creation. I love each of you so much.

Thank you to my husband, Neil. You have been my biggest supporter throughout this process. I love you more!

Rosie's Regret

ISBN: 978-0-578-54692-6

Library of Congress Control Number: 2019910055

Front cover image, illustrations, and book design by Nicole Filippone

First printing edition 2019

Rosie's Regret

Written by Amy Lindley
Illustrated by Nicole Filippone

Rosie spent all day getting ready for her extra-special birthday party. She had waited four years for this birthday and today was her **big day**!

She had patiently watched as her mother, father, grandma, grandpa, aunts, cousins, and friends all had their birthdays...

and now, finally, today was
her special day!

Rosie carefully placed all the matching cups, plates, and napkins on the table, which sat outside on a warm October afternoon.

All her outdoor toys were placed in the yard for her guests to
play with, including her favorite red crawl through tunnel.
She waited ever so patiently for her guests to arrive.

Sarah was the first guest to appear and Rosie was so excited to see her best friend.

"Hi Rosie," said Sarah happily. "I just know you are going to love this present!"

Sarah was holding a rectangle-shaped box, loosely wrapped as if she had wrapped it herself.

"Put it on the table and let's go swing!" said Rosie.

Sarah and Rosie played on the swing set until all her guests arrived.

"It's painting time," announced Rosie. Rosie's mom placed white star boxes and individual packs of paint at everyone's seat.

As everyone began creating their own magic star, Sarah said again, "Hey Rosie, you are really going to like the present I got you. I picked it out myself!"

"We will open presents after the cake!" said Rosie as she continued to paint her star box with sparkles and glitter.

When everyone had finished painting their stars, Rosie's mom put them in the sun to dry.

Michael's was the prettiest, but that's because he had just turned five.

"Okay, come stand around the cake table," directed Rosie's mom.

"Rosie, you stand on the chair so you can blow out your candles."

Rosie climbed up the wooden chair excited to see her brightly decorated cake.

The sound of everyone singing was so overwhelming that Rosie blew out her candles before the song was finished.

Hap-py birth-day
to
you!

Finally, it was time for the presents! Sarah, Michael, Jalen, and Shelby all gathered around Rosie's chair while she opened the first gift. It was a brand-new doll from Shelby. "Thank you, Shelby," said Rosie.

Rosie continued to open her presents until she finally got to Sarah's rectangle shaped box.

Rosie slowly peeled the glossy striped paper away revealing a Candy World board game. "Oh man, I already have this," declared Rosie. Sarah's joyous face turned upside down and a tear began to form in her eye.

"Rosie!" said her mother sternly.

But it was too late. Sarah's feelings were already hurt.

CANDY WORLD

Later that night, after all her guests had departed and everything except the balloons had been put away, Rosie asked her mom what she should do to make Sarah feel better.

"Rosie, you should have smiled and said thank you even though you already have the game. It's more important to make your friend feel appreciated. And, we can always exchange it for something you do not have later."

"Alright, mom. But, how do I make Sarah feel better now?"

"Well, what if you call Sarah and ask her to go with you to the toy store and help you pick out a new toy?" asked mom.

"That's a great idea! And, you know what else I can do?" suggested Rosie. "I can say I'm sorry."

"You are a very smart little girl," said mom proudly.

"I'm not little anymore, mom. I'm four!" said Rosie.

Rosie did exactly what her mom suggested, and Sarah was happy to go shopping with her best friend.

"I was upset, but when you said that you were sorry, it made me feel better," said Sarah as they both galloped down the doll aisle.

Rosie learned that it is important to make her friends feel happy and to always be polite when someone gives her a gift!

I'll remember what to do the next time I open a present!

The End

About the Author

Amy Lindley grew up in Greensboro, NC where she taught elementary school and received her M.Ed in education. She now lives and teaches in Wilmington, NC with her husband and five children. She wrote "Rosie's Regret" after taking her daughter to a birthday party where the birthday girl inadvertently hurt another child's feelings when opening gifts. She wanted to teach her daughter what to do if the same situation happened to her.

Made in the USA
Columbia, SC
25 September 2019